Air Power

F-35 LIGHTNING II

MEGAN COOLEY PETERSON

BLACK RABBIT BOOKS

BOLT

Bolt is published by Black Rabbit Books
P.O. Box 3263, Mankato, Minnesota, 56002.
www.blackrabbitbooks.com

Jennifer Besel, editor; Grant Gould & Michael Sellner, designers; Omay Ayres, photo researcher

Library of Congress Cataloging-in-Publication Data
Names: Peterson, Megan Cooley, author.
Title: F-35 Lightning II / by Megan Cooley Peterson.
Description: Mankato, Minnesota : Black Rabbit Books, [2019] | Series: Bolt. Air power | Includes bibliographical references and index. | Audience: Grades 4-6. | Audience: Ages 9-12.
Identifiers: LCCN 2017025354 (print) | LCCN 2017026165 (ebook) | ISBN 9781680725001 (ebook) | ISBN 9781680723847 (library binding) | ISBN 9781680726787 (paperback)
Subjects: LCSH: F-35 (Military aircraft)—Juvenile literature.
Classification: LCC UG1242.F5 (ebook) | LCC UG1242.F5 P4734 2019 (print) | DDC 358.4/383—dc23
LC record available at https://lccn.loc.gov/2017025354

Printed in China. 3/18

Image Credits

af.mil: US Air Force/Tom Reynolds, 26; Alamy: US Marines Photo, 20 (b); commons.wikimedia.org: Ahunt, 32; defenseimagery.mil, US Air Force/Master Sgt John Nimmo Sr., 13, 22–23; .mil, US Department of Defense, 14 (b); defense.gov: US Air Force/R. Nial Bradshaw, 28–29; US Air Force/Senior Airman Thomas Spangler, 27; US Department of Defense, 6–7, 31; Dreamstime: Anton Barashenkov, 24; Digitalstormcinema, 20 (t); eglin.af.mil: US Air Force Photo, Cover; flickr.com: ermaleksandr, 16; Lockheed Martin/Aeronautica Militare: 15 (t); misawa.af.mil: US Air Force/Airman 1st Class Patrick S. Ciccarone, 25; navy.mil: US Air Force Photo/Samuel King Jr., 15 (b); US Navy/Chief Mass Communication Specialist Eric A. Clement, 14 (t); nellis.af.mil: US Air Force//Lawrence Crespo, 4–5; rockwellcollins.com: Rockwell Collins, 3, 19; Shutterstock: Charles F McCarthy, 9 (b); Digital Storm, 21; Guillermo Pis Gonzalez, 9 (m); MyImages - Micha, 1, 14–15 (bkgd); Soonthorn Wongsaita, 9 (t); WindVector, 19; the-blueprints.com: The Blue-prints, 10–11; wpafb.af.mil: US Air Force/Derek Kaufman, 18

CONTENTS

CHAPTER 1
Flying into the Unknown. 4

CHAPTER 2
History of the F-35. 8

CHAPTER 3
F-35 Lightning II Features. 17

CHAPTER 4
The F-35 Lightning II in Action. 24

Other Resources. 30

CHAPTER 1

FLYING into the Unknown

It was a cool morning. Tom Morgenfeld slid into the **cockpit** of an F-35 Lightning II. The fighter jet was about to fly for the first time.

RESCUE

The F-35's first flight lasted 22 minutes.

A Fun First Flight

Morgenfeld guided the plane up to 10,000 feet (3,048 meters). He looped figure eights. Morgenfeld was thrilled with the plane. He wanted to fly longer!

CHAPTER 2

HISTORY of the F-35

In the 1990s, U.S. fighter jets were getting old. They weren't fast enough. Enemy **radar** could track them.

The U.S. Air Force, Marine Corps, and Navy also flew different jets. They wanted one fighter each branch could use. The military held a contest to find a new plane.

AIR FORCE'S F-16 FIGHTING FALCON

MARINES' AV-8 HARRIER JUMP JET

NAVY'S F-18 HORNET

Winning the Contest

The Lockheed Martin and Boeing companies competed. They each built a new jet. Lockheed's design won. It had better **vertical** landing.

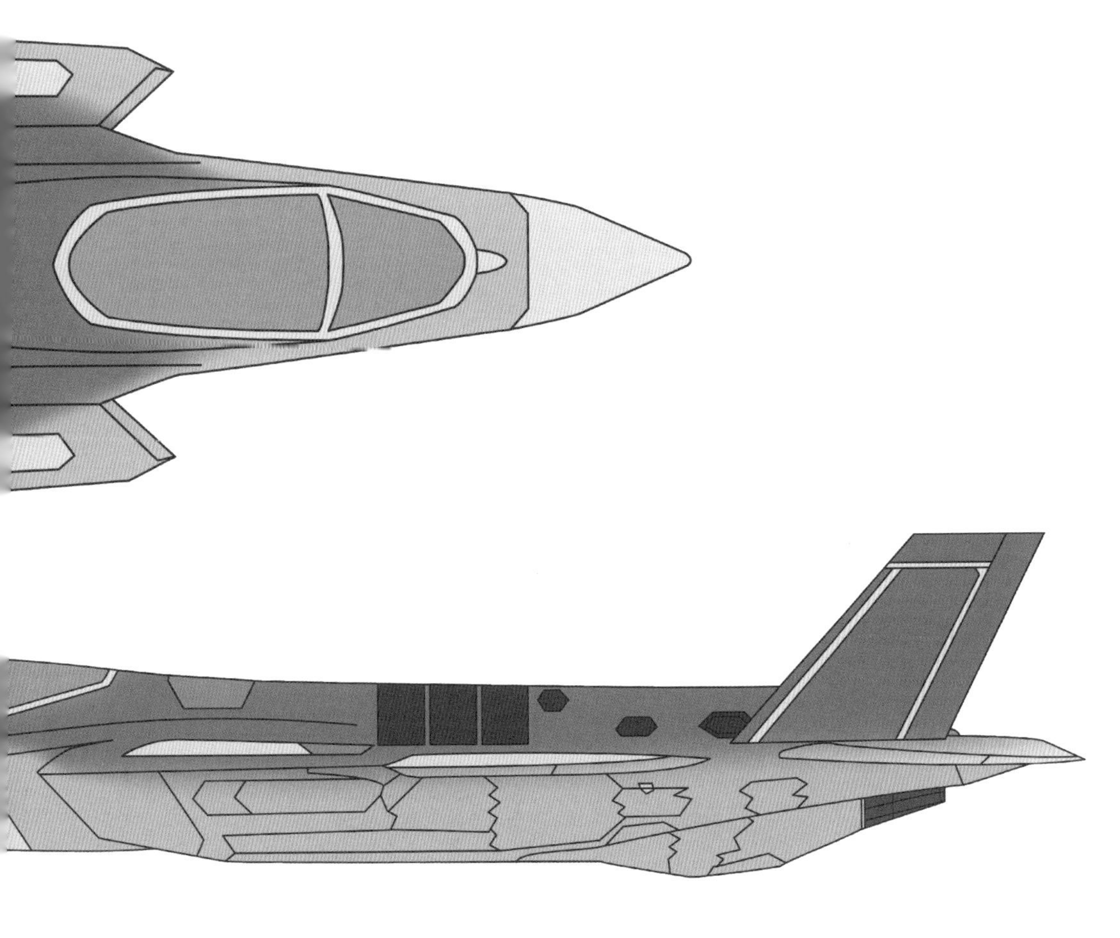

Making Three Versions

The U.S. Army, Navy, and Marines had different needs. Other countries also wanted the plane. Design changes slowed the project. It also added millions of dollars to the cost. Finally, engineers made three different F-35s.

	wingspan	weight (empty)
F-35A	35 feet (11 m)	29,300 pounds (13,290 kilograms)
F-35B	35 feet (11 m)	32,300 pounds (14,651 kg)
F-35C	43 feet (13 m)	34,800 pounds (15,785 kg)

F-35B
7
14
21
28
35
42
49
5,000
10,000
15,000
20,000
25,000
30,000
35,000

F-35 LIGHTNING II TIMELINE

2001
Lockheed's design wins the contest.

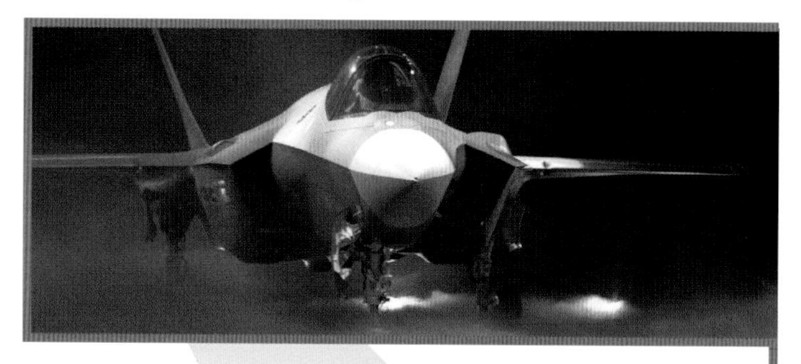

1990

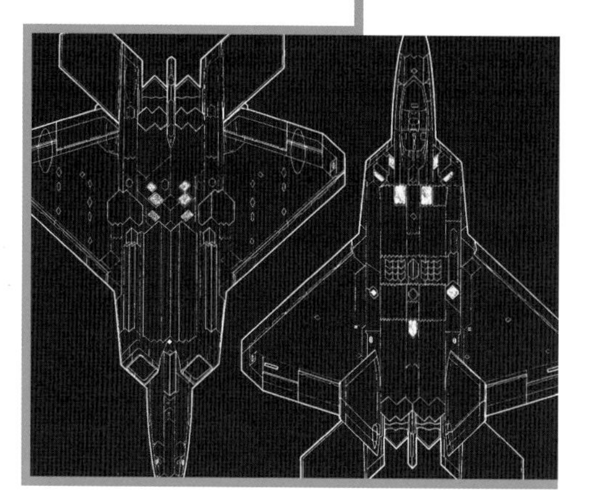

1997
Companies compete to build new fighters.

2015

The F-35B is **combat** ready.

2016

The F-35A is combat ready.

2019

The F-35C is expected to be combat ready.

CHAPTER 3

F-35 Lightning II FEATURES

Don't blink! The F-35 flies up to 1,200 miles (1,931 km) per hour. That's faster than the speed of sound!

The F-35 has a smooth shape. It carries weapons inside the plane. These features help the plane slip past radar.

A Great View

Each F-35 pilot wears a high-tech helmet. Cameras outside the plane send images to the helmet. The pilot can see all around the plane.

The plane's technology also senses problems. It tells pilots which problems to handle first. No other airplane has this technology.

More than 500 U.S. pilots are trained to fly the F-35. They train using simulators.

3 X
TIME:
ALTITUDE:

Three F-35s

F-35A
used by U.S. Air Force, Canada, and several other countries

F-35B
used by U.S. Marines and United Kingdom

F-35C
to be used by U.S. Navy

A, B, and C

The three F-35s have different features. The F-35A takes off and lands like a regular plane. It also has a cannon. The F-35B has short takeoffs and vertical landings. The F-35C has larger wings. It is built to land on **aircraft carriers**.

F-35 LIGHTNING II PARTS

ENGINE
WING
MISSILE STORAGE
(INSIDE THE PLANE)

CHAPTER 4

The F-35 Lightning II in ACTION

The F-35 attacks without being seen. **Sensors** jam enemy radar. They also scan for other planes.

F-35s are the first wave of attack. They clear the way for other aircraft. They shoot planes in the air. They also destroy ground targets.

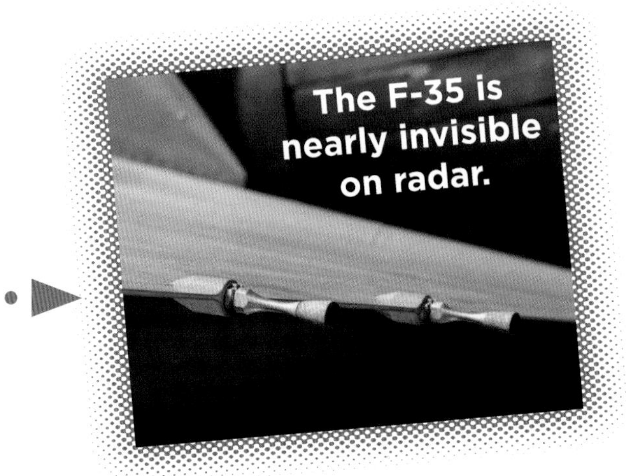
The F-35 is nearly invisible on radar.

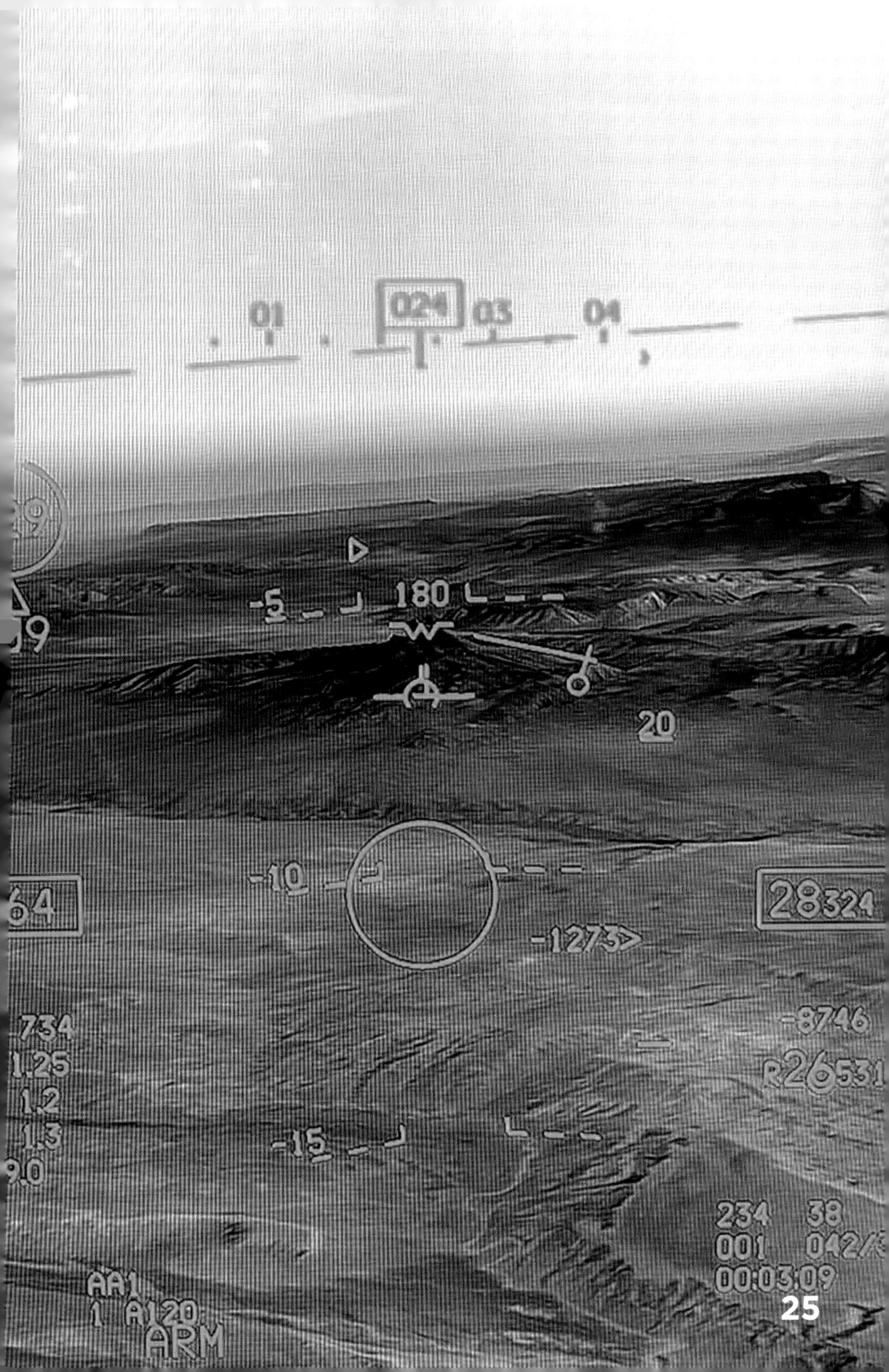
024
01
03
04
180
-5
20
-10
-1273
-8746
734
1.25
1.2
1.3
-15
234
38
001
00:03:09
AA1
1 A120
ARM

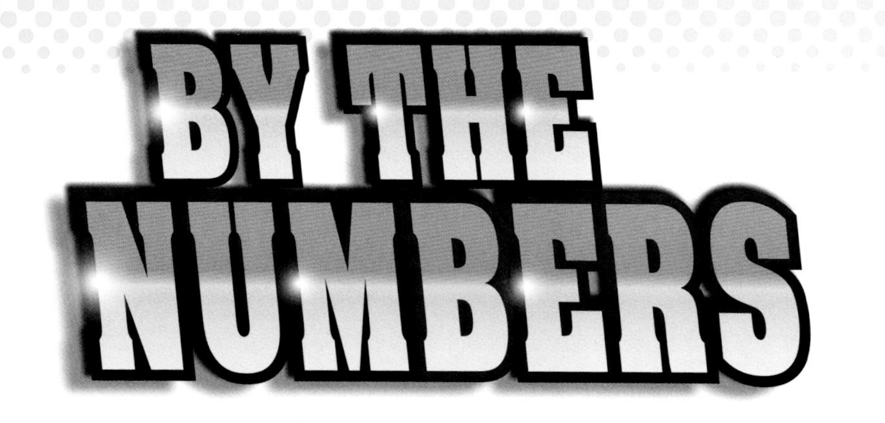

400 BILLION

number of jobs the plane's processor can do each second

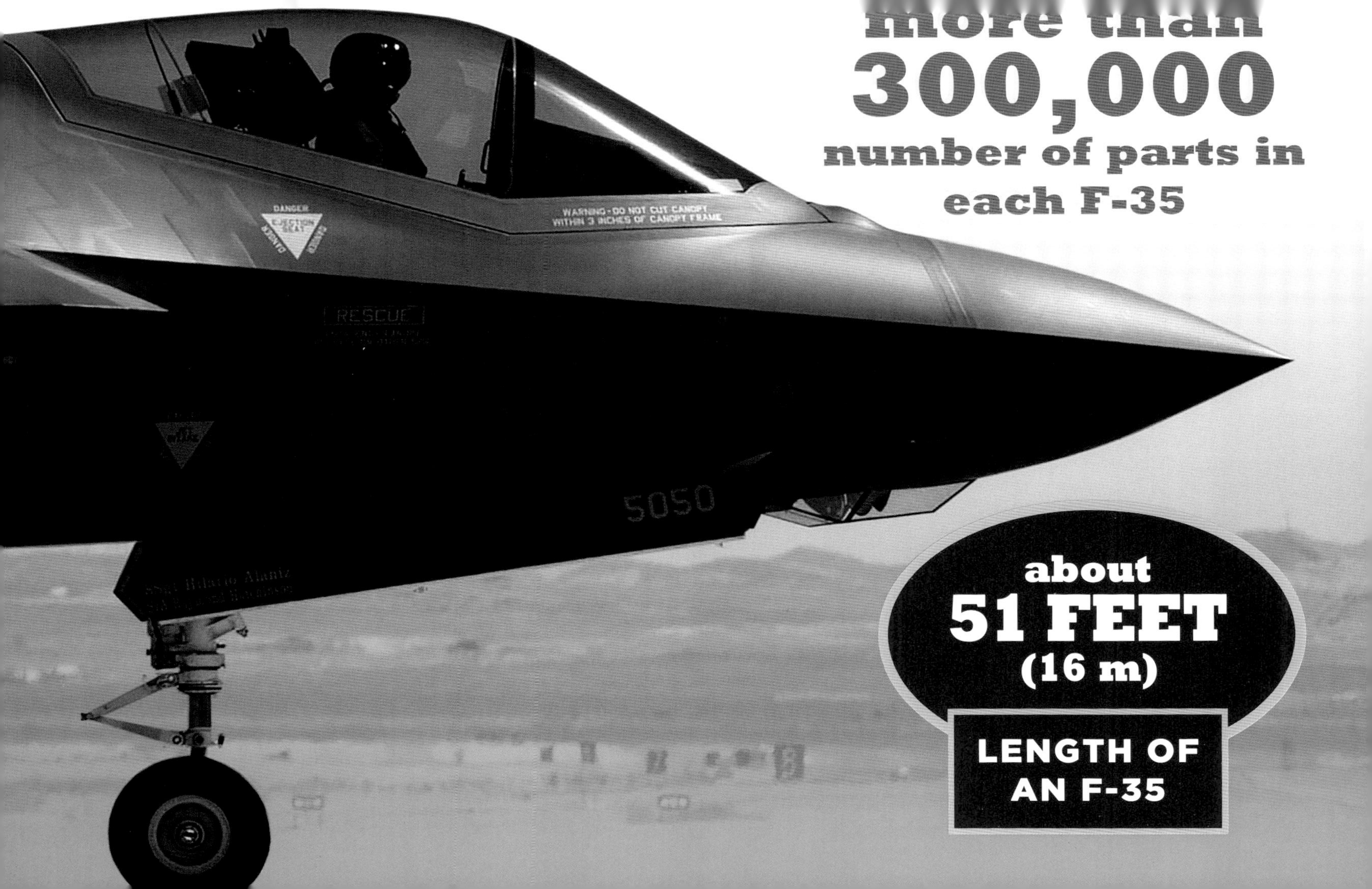

more than
300,000
number of parts in
each F-35
DANGER
EJECTION SEAT
WARNING - DO NOT CUT CANOPY WITHIN 3 INCHES OF CANOPY FRAME
RESCUE
5050
about
51 FEET
(16 m)
LENGTH OF
AN F-35

Fighter of the Future

The F-35 is a game-changing fighter. No other plane can do what it does. The F-35 will shape warfare for years to come.

HL
HL
388 FW
HL

aircraft carrier (AIR-kraft KAR-ee-uhr)—a warship with a large flat deck where aircraft take off and land

cockpit (KOK-pit)—the area in a boat, plane, or car where a driver sits

combat (kahm-BAT)—active fighting, often in a war

processor (PRAH-seh-sur)—a part of a computer that processes data

radar (RAY-dar)—a device that sends out radio waves for finding the location and speed of a moving object

sensor (SEN-sor)—a device that finds heat, light, sound, motion, or other things

simulator (SIM-yuh-lay-tuhr)—a device that lets the user practice under test conditions

vertical (VUR-tuh-kuhl)—straight up and down

BOOKS

Nagelhout, Ryan. *Fighter Planes.* Mighty Military Machines. New York: Gareth Stevens Publishing, 2015.

Oxlade, Chris. *Inside Fighter Planes.* Inside Military Machines. Minneapolis: Hungry Tomato, 2018.

Willis, John. *Fighter Jets.* Mighty Military Machines. New York: AV2 by Weigl, 2017.

WEBSITES

F-35A Lightning II
www.af.mil/AboutUs/FactSheets/Display/tabid/224/Article/478441/f-35a-lightning-ii-conventional-takeoff-and-landing-variant.aspx

F-35 Lightning II
www.f35.com

F-35 Lightning II
www.lockheedmartin.com/us/products/f35.html

INDEX

C

costs, 12, 26

H

history, 8, 11,
12, 14–15

P

pilots, 18

processors, 26

R

radar, 8, 17, 24

S

sizes, 12–13, 27

speeds, 17

V

variations, 12–13, 15, 20–21

W

weapons, 17, 21, 23